The Puppies of Blossom Meadow

The Puppies of Blossom Meadow

By Catherine Coe

Book 2:
Mischief and Magic

SCHOLASTIC

Published in the UK by Scholastic Children's Books, 2021
Euston House, 24 Eversholt Street, London, NW1 1DB, UK
A division of Scholastic Limited.

Scholastic Ltd Ireland Offices at:
Unit 89E, Lagan Road, Dublin Industrial Estate, Glasnevin, Dublin 11

SCHOLASTIC and associated logos are trademarks and/or
registered trademarks of Scholastic Inc.

ISBN 978 1407 19867 5

A CIP catalogue record for this book
is available from the British Library.

Printed by CPI Group (UK) Ltd, Croydon, CR0 4YY

Papers used by Scholastic Children's Books are made
from wood grown in sustainable forests and other controlled sources.

1 3 5 7 9 10 8 6 4 2

www.scholastic.co.uk

Also by Catherine Coe

The Owls of Blossom Wood

A Magical Beginning
To the Rescue
Lost and Found
The Birthday Party
Save the Day
An Enchanted Wedding

The Unicorns of Blossom Wood

Believe in Magic
Festival Time
Storms and Rainbows
Best Friends

The Puppies of Blossom Meadow

Fairy Friends
Mischief and Magic

For Matt xxx
(Yes, the sausage dog was
named after you!)

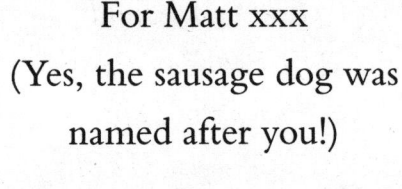

Chapter 1

Walkies!

Ding-ding, dong-dong!

At the sound of the doorbell, Amber hopped to the front door with just one shoe on. She'd spent the last ten minutes looking everywhere for the other one.

She opened the door to Erin, Kayla and Kayla's dad. "I'm almost ready!" Amber said. "But I've lost a trainer..."

"Can't you wear some other shoes?" Erin suggested. She was desperate to get to Doggy Delights, where the three best friends would be helping out again, just like yesterday.

Amber shook her head. "I need trainers on if we're going to take the dogs for a walk!"

"You could always hop all day," Kayla joked.

Amber frowned as if she was considering that for a moment when her mum rushed into the hallway, holding up a blue-and-white shoe. "It was in the kitchen, Amber," her mum said. "I had to replace the broken lace, remember?"

"Thanks, Mum!" Amber grinned. She shoved the trainer on and tied the laces in a double knot. "Ready!" she told her friends.

They waved at Amber's mum as Amber

stepped outside to the walkway of the block
of flats. Erin and Kayla gave her a quick
hug and then they followed Kayla's dad
down the stairs to the ground floor. The
girls lived in the same block of flats: Amber
was on the first floor, Erin lived on the
fifth and Kayla on the seventh.

"I can't wait to see all the dogs again!"
said Kayla, skipping out on to the
pavement.

"And go back to Blossom Meadow!" Erin said, not very quietly. Kayla looked over at her dad, worrying that he might have heard, but he was busy looking up and down the road, checking for traffic.

Amber bit her lip. "But what if we can't?" she said. "Maybe yesterday was a one-off!"

Yesterday, they'd found a magical collar in the storeroom at Doggy Delights – the dog kennels where Kayla's dad worked. When they touched it, they had been whisked off to Blossom Meadow, where they were no longer girls but puppies. They'd met lots of friendly animals, birds and insects, and had the most magical adventure, helping out the fairies who lived in the bluebells.

"We'll just have to wait and see," whispered Kayla as they crossed the road.

After walking for another ten minutes, they arrived at the door of Doggy Delights. It looked just like a normal Victorian house from the outside, but inside it was filled with dogs of all shapes and sizes!

A German shepherd scampered into the hallway and licked Kayla's hand. "Hello, Poppy!" Kayla said.

Amber and Erin bent down to stroke a

sausage dog and a beagle that had rushed straight up to them.

"It looks as if the dogs have chosen their walkers for today already!" Kayla's dad said, smiling. "We're going to do the morning walks first thing for a change, so let's get their leads on."

Erin, Kayla and Amber looked at each other. They'd been hoping to get to the storeroom to find the magical collar right away!

Kayla's dad's smile turned into a frown. "What's wrong? Yesterday you couldn't wait to take the dogs out for their walk."

"Nothing, Dad!" Kayla said, grabbing Poppy's lead from the shelf. She *was* excited about doing a dog walk. Just not quite as excited as she was by the thought of going back to Blossom Meadow!

Kayla's dad passed the beagle's lead to

Erin. "This is for Toto," he said, "and this is for Matt." He passed another lead to Amber, which she clipped on to the sausage dog. "I checked with their owners," he went on, "and they are happy for you to walk the dogs yourselves, as long as I'm with you."

Amber bounced up and down. "Really? That's so cool!"

Yesterday Kayla's dad had held the leads while the three best friends walked beside him. But now they would each get to look after a dog properly. They couldn't have pets in the block of flats they lived in, so this was the next best thing!

They took the dogs to a park just around the corner. Kayla's dad held on to five dogs, and each of them seemed to want to go in a different direction. Kayla couldn't help but laugh as her dad spun around, trying to untangle the leads and guide the dogs the same way. Happily, her dog, Poppy, was very calm, and didn't pull on the lead at all.

Once they reached the dog area in the park and shut the gate behind them, they took the dogs off their leads. The friends grinned as the dogs chased each other back and forth, and Kayla's dad threw some balls for them to run after.

"When are we going to get back to

Doggy Delights?" Erin asked. "I want to find the collar and go to Blossom Meadow again!"

Amber shrugged as she launched one of the balls to the other side of the area and ran after it.

Kayla giggled. "It's not you who's supposed to chase it, Amber!"

"I know, but it's fun," Amber replied, her long legs sprinting across the grass.

After the dogs – and Amber – had run around for half an hour, Kayla's dad began clipping the leads on the dogs again. "We should head back now. There's a doggy groomer coming in today, and we don't want to miss that."

Erin turned to her friends. They were never going to get back to Blossom Meadow at this rate! They needed to get to the storeroom – but how? As she fastened Toto's lead, she blurted, "Don't you need anything from the storeroom today? We could tidy it again!"

Kayla's dad looked at Erin strangely. "I didn't think you enjoyed doing that! But actually, you've reminded me – we need to bring in some new bags of dry dog food. It'd be great if you girls can fetch some as soon as we get back."

Erin breathed a sigh of relief and almost

ran to Doggy Delights. Toto scampered along, trying to keep up with her, with Amber, Matt, Kayla and Poppy not far behind. Kayla's dad was lagging at the back of the group, getting even more twisted up in the dog leads than he had on their way there!

As soon as they reached Doggy Delights, Amber, Kayla and Erin ran out to the storeroom.

"Where was the collar before?" Amber said. "Was it on a shelf?"

"No!" said Erin. "It was on top of the cupboard. Don't you remember? You were the one who found it!"

"You're so forgetful," Kayla said, "but we still love you!" She squeezed her friend's arm as Erin reached up to the top of the cupboard and felt around. But she was too short to see, and at first it seemed as if nothing was there. Her heart began to beat harder. "It's gone!"

Amber came over and stretched up on to her tiptoes. She was the tallest of the three friends, which often came in handy. "Wait! I see it!"

She took down the purple collar, which sparkled as it moved. The girls smiled at the sight of the Blossom name tag spinning on its little chain. Would it take them on another adventure?

"Now what?" Amber said.

"We hold on to it together, just like last time!" Erin said, grabbing it impatiently.

Amber let go and put her hands to her face. "But Kayla's dad will wonder where we are. He's expecting us back with the dog food!"

Kayla reached out for the collar as the silver Blossom name tag spun around. "It doesn't matter! No time passed here the last time we were in Blossom Meadow. Quick, Amber, grab the collar – I don't want to leave you behind!"

"Oh, yeah, I remember now," said Amber, and snapped her hand out to take hold of the collar again. Now all three girls were touching it, white sparkles began zipping off its surface, whipping around them in a circle. The next moment, their feet were lifting off the floor and they rose higher and higher into the air.

Kayla looked down, but she couldn't even see the ground or her feet now – the sparkles were as thick as a dust storm in the desert. Her skin shivered and her ears popped as she blinked again and again.

Amber closed her eyes and tried not

to scream. It wasn't that she was scared, but it felt strange to be surrounded by so much magic. Soon they'd be in Blossom Meadow – at least, she hoped they would!

Chapter 2

Back in Blossom Meadow

Moments later, Erin felt her feet land on solid ground. The whirling sparkles began to fade away until she could see two puppies beside her. There was a sleek black terrier with a white stomach, which she knew from last time was Amber, and a fluffy brown cockapoo, which was Kayla. Erin knew she'd be a golden Labrador, but she double-checked anyway with a quick look at her little pale yellow paws and golden wagging tail.

"We've arrived in the poppy field this time!" said Kayla, looking around, her brown nose twitching. They were surrounded by waving orange poppies, double the height of the puppies. The first time they'd come to Blossom Meadow, they'd landed in a field full of tiny white daisies.

"What should we do first?" Amber wondered as she scooped the magic collar on to her neck for safekeeping. She hopped from paw to paw, her tail swishing like a windscreen wiper.

Erin spun around in a blur of golden fur. "It's the fairy twins' birthday today! And they invited us to their party, remember?"

"Oh, yes, we must go and wish them happy birthday," Kayla barked as she nodded her furry brown head. She hoped the twins were having a good birthday — and that no one had picked their precious bluebells overnight! Yesterday, the friends had done their best to persuade the residents of Blossom Meadow that they should only pick flowers that grew back quickly, but she didn't know the creatures here well enough yet to be sure they would have listened.

"Maybe we'll be able to have another wish cake!" said Amber, still bouncing about on her paws. Last time, the fairies had given them each a fairy cake and told them to make a wish. And all of their wishes had come true, including Kayla's – which had been to return to Blossom Meadow!

"That would be awesome," Erin said, already thinking about what she might wish.

Kayla jumped up and down on her hind

legs, trying to see higher than the poppies. "Which way is Bluebell Grove?" she asked.

"Don't ask me," said Amber. She could never remember directions. Amber had lost count of the number of times she'd got lost on the way to Erin's flat – even though she lived in the same block and had been there hundreds of times!

"I remember!" Erin sniffed her nose into the air. "We need to get to the Badger Burrows first, and by the smell coming from over there, I think it's *that* way!" She pointed to their right with her paw and began to scamper away, between the poppy stems. Kayla and Amber followed just behind her, taking care not to trample any flowers as they went.

They soon reached a large patch of brown soil, dotted with burrow holes.

"Hey, there's George!" Kayla said, running over to a large badger who was lumbering towards the far side of the burrows. "George," she called, and the badger stopped, turned around and squinted at them.

"It's us!" Erin said. "The puppies!" All three of them raced over to George, who beamed at them and waved.

"Oh, it's marvellous to see you three back in the meadow," he said in his deep voice. "But I'm afraid I can't stop – I'm off to visit my cousin over in Blossom Wood, and I'm already running dreadfully late!"

"No worries," said Kayla. "We just wanted to say hi. We're on our way to visit the fairies in Bluebell Grove."

George nodded. "Well, have a lovely time. Just don't go anywhere near

Buttercup Bridge today!"

"Why is that?" Erin asked.

The badger peered at a watch on his left wrist. "Oh dear, I really don't have time to explain. Just take my word for it, please!" He gave another quick wave and hurried off, faster than they'd ever seen him move before.

"I wonder what's wrong with Buttercup Bridge," said Amber.

Erin's pale yellow ears waggled with

worry. "We need to cross it to get to Bluebell Grove. I don't know any other way there!"

"But George seemed very certain we shouldn't go near it," Kayla replied.

"How bad can it be?" said Erin. She was determined to get to the fairies today. "If we run fast, we'll be over it in a couple of seconds!"

Amber's tail dropped. "I really don't think we should, Erin."

Kayla looked around. There were no other badgers in sight, but there had to be other creatures nearby. "Let's try to speak to someone else," she suggested. "Someone who isn't in quite such a hurry. They might be able to tell us what George meant."

"Good idea," Amber replied, her tail lifting again.

"OK," said Erin. "But if we can't find anyone soon, I think we should risk it!"

They had just reached the edge of the Badger Burrows by Violet Green when they spotted the deer and her fawn that they'd given wildflowers to yesterday.

"Hello, puppies," the deer said as Kayla, Erin and Amber scampered up to her. "Thank you again for the flowers. We haven't picked any bluebells at all, don't worry!"

"Thank you—" Amber began.

"What's wrong with Buttercup Bridge?" Erin blurted out, accidentally interrupting her friend.

The wide-eyed fawn suddenly burst into tears and her mother put a hoof around her to comfort her.

"Oh, please don't mention that place

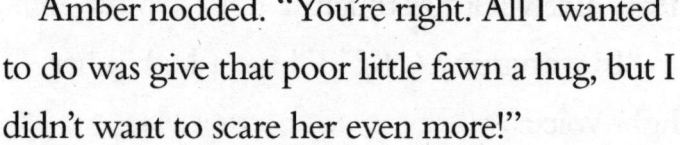

today," the deer said. She turned to her fawn.
"Come along now, don't cry, sweetie." She
guided her away, and waved goodbye to the
puppies.

"I didn't mean to upset the fawn," Erin
said, feeling shocked.

"We know you didn't," Kayla told her,
putting a paw on her friend's shoulder. "But
it must be something serious at Buttercup
Bridge for the fawn to react like that."

Amber nodded. "You're right. All I wanted
to do was give that poor little fawn a hug, but I
didn't want to scare her even more!"

They wandered into Violet Green, but didn't dare go too close to Buttercup Bridge on the other side. Amber looked around carefully for any creatures who might be able to tell them what was wrong, but when she called out to a couple of ants scuttling along the ground, they only rushed away even faster.

"Look!" Kayla said suddenly. "There's Chloe!"

A purple-tipped butterfly zoomed across the sky above them, casting the tiniest shadow on the ground. "Chloe!" Erin barked, her voice booming out across the meadow. The butterfly stopped in mid-air, changing her direction to shoot towards the ground. She slowed down as she drew near, so that when she landed on Erin's shoulder, Erin barely felt her touch.

"Is everything OK?" Chloe asked in her light voice.

All three puppies shook their heads. "Not really," said Amber. "We're trying to find out what's wrong with Buttercup Bridge. Do you know?"

Chloe hung her head. "Oh, puppies, it's awful!" she said. "One of the trolls is behaving very badly. And I hate to see everyone in Blossom Meadow upset!"

Kayla twitched her nose. "What do you mean? What's the troll doing?"

The butterfly lifted her head again and
sighed. "I think the best way is to show you.
Follow me..."

Chapter 3

Behaving Badly

The puppies scampered across Violet
Green, keeping Chloe in their sights just
above them. It wasn't long before they got
to the very edge of the field. The puppies
stopped as Chloe flew down towards a
particularly thick clump of violets.

"Let's hide here," the butterfly
whispered, her voice so light that even the

puppies, with their excellent hearing, could hardly make it out. "Can you see Buttercup Bridge?"

Amber, Kayla and Erin nodded. "So where's the troll?" Erin asked, squinting through the wildflowers.

Chloe made a squeaking sound. "Please keep your voices down," she whispered. The butterfly pointed a wing at the bridge in the distance. "And please make sure you stay hidden!"

The puppies stared, barely blinking, waiting to see what the problem was. Amber had to concentrate on all of her paws to stop them bouncing about like they usually did.

Erin tried her best to stay still, but her golden ears still twitched occasionally. She often had trouble keeping quiet and not moving – school assemblies were the worst when she always seemed to get a sneezing fit or itchy feet.

At last, something moved near Buttercup Bridge. Kayla held her breath as she watched some little creatures dart towards the bridge, quickly realizing it was a family of tawny-brown mice. When they were about a metre from the bridge, right before the carpet of buttercups began, a creature jumped up from the stream below, back-flipping on to the bridge like an acrobat. When he came to a standstill, Kayla took in his appearance – a large grey head, big pointy ears, green eyes and shoulder-length blonde hair. He was wearing brown dungarees that were covered in patches and long, dark-green shoes that looked a bit like a clown's.

Kayla let out her breath. He didn't look very scary. In fact, his rosy cheeks and dimples made him look really quite friendly.

Then he opened his mouth to speak.

"Payment for your crossing," the troll growled. Amber bit her lip. His voice

sounded similar to the grumpy old man's who lived in the flat below hers. He always complained when Amber played music, even when the volume was super quiet.

The mice had stopped and the largest mouse stood on tiptoes. "Mr Troll, I'm afraid we don't have anything to pay you. Please will you let us cross? We're on our way to visit our cousins on Lupin Lane." Her voice grew higher and higher and squeakier and squeakier with every word.

Erin guessed this was the mother mouse. It took absolutely all of her willpower not to scamper over there and tell the troll to pick on creatures his own size.

The troll let out a long, deep growl and the mice jumped back as one. "Nothing to pay me? I can see you have something right there," the troll bellowed. "That sack of cheese will do nicely!"

"B–b–but, Mr Troll," the mother mouse said. "This will feed our f–f–family for a week. It's nothing to you. Please let us keep it!"

"No cheese, no crossing," the troll said. "It's your choice!" He planted his feet wide, at either side of the bridge. Kayla wondered whether the mice would make a run for it between his legs, but of course they didn't.

The mouse with the sack of cheese on his back dropped it on the ground in front of the troll. The troll took one giant step forward, scooped up the sack and somersaulted back into the stream.

"Now you may pass," he growled as he disappeared under the bridge with a splash and a gurgle. The mice ran over the wooden bridge, their tiny feet making a plinking sound as they crossed the rickety beams.

Back on Violet Green, Chloe turned to the puppies. "Trudge has been terrorizing anyone who wants to use the bridge since first light this morning. It's dreadful!" Tears sprang to her eyes as she fluttered her wings in despair.

Kayla's ears flapped with confusion. "Isn't that what trolls usually do? At least, they do in the stories I've read!"

"Oh no," Chloe replied. "The trolls of Blossom Meadow are normally kind and friendly. They wouldn't be allowed to live here otherwise!"

Amber immediately felt bad for all trolls everywhere. It wasn't fair that books made them out to be horrible creatures, when not all of them were.

"It's all right for butterflies like me," Chloe went on, "and birds and other insects that can fly. But it's terrible for anyone who has to walk across. They can only get over by giving something to Trudge. And that's just not fair!"

Erin agreed. It wasn't fair at all! That made up her mind. With fury in her eyes and a thumping heart, she dodged around Kayla, Amber and Chloe, and sprinted towards Buttercup Bridge before anyone could stop her.

Chapter 4

Trudge and Trim

"Hey, troll!" Erin shouted as she reached the thick patch of buttercups at the approach to the bridge. "I'd like to speak to you."

Trudge leapt up on to Buttercup Bridge, this time landing on the railing, where he sat, swinging his legs. "Payment for your crossing," he growled just like before. He held out a large grey palm and Erin noticed his grey fingernails were all bitten down.

"I'm not here to cross the bridge," Erin barked. "I want to talk to you about what you're doing!"

Back in the violet field, Amber bounced up and down with worry. "Should we go over?" she whispered to Kayla.

Kayla wasn't sure. Erin often didn't think before she spoke, and she was worried that her friend's impulsiveness might get her in trouble now. But Erin was also determined and brave – so maybe she could change the troll's mind. She listened to what Erin was saying next.

"It's not fair for you to demand payment from anyone who wants to cross the bridge," Erin told Trudge. "You took all the food off those poor mice!"

The troll glared at the Labrador. "Mice,

lice, smice! It's the trolls' bridge. So it's our rules. Like it or leave it!"

"But—" Erin started.

"But nothing," Trudge interrupted her. "Now, if you're not going to pay me to cross the bridge, go away!"

Erin stared at the troll, as if that might change his mind, but he just stared back with his emerald-green eyes. He didn't seem to blink at all!

Erin sighed, turned around and scampered back to her friends.

"Well done for trying," Chloe said.

"Maybe he'll think about what you said," Kayla added, trying to stay positive. "It might just take him a while to realize what he's doing is wrong."

Amber shuffled from paw to paw. "I don't know," she said nervously. "He seemed pretty certain."

Erin had to agree. It hadn't worked at all. Now what would they do?

Chloe tried to smile. "How about you come back to mine for some raspberry tea?" she suggested. "A cup of something warm and sweet always makes me feel better."

The three puppies nodded. Amber didn't think there was any point in staying here. Kayla needed time to think, and a cup of raspberry tea sounded delicious. Meanwhile Erin wondered just where a butterfly would live. In a tree like a bird, or amongst flower stems like the fairies?

It turned out it was neither of those places. After they'd raced back across Violet Green, Chloe turned left into Daisy Heath and fluttered to a stop by a line of raspberry bushes that bordered the heath and the meadow. The branches were heavy with giant, ripe raspberries, and Kayla's mouth watered at the sight of them.

Chloe must have seen her face. "Please try one," Chloe told Kayla. "You too, Erin and Amber. You won't find a more delicious raspberry anywhere!"

Kayla and Erin each plucked a raspberry from the bush, and a burst of sweet, fruity flavour filled their mouths. But Amber held back. She could never eat anything when she was worried, whereas the bigger the problem, the more Kayla seemed to eat.

"You're missing out!" Erin said to Amber, as pink raspberry juice dribbled down her golden chin.

"Maybe later," Amber replied.

Chloe beckoned them with her wing towards a gap in the hedge. "Watch out for thorns!" she said. "I try to remove the thorns as soon as I see them, but I miss the odd pesky one occasionally."

They followed the little butterfly through the green outer leaves and into the shadowy, cooler heart of the raspberry bush. It was lucky that they were all small puppies, and could squeeze inside without damaging the branches.

In the middle of the bush, the branches opened out to a circular home, complete with a dining table with a leaf tablecloth, a

bed with a daisy blanket and a rug of woven grasses. The puppies did their best to sit around the dining table, but Kayla guessed it was really meant for much smaller creatures.

Chloe fluttered over, carrying four chestnut cups filled with steaming tea. "Be careful — it's hot!" she said.

"Thank you," Kayla said, breathing in the warm fruity smell from the cup in front of her.

Amber picked up her cup but nearly dropped it again when Erin shouted, "It's still hot, Amber!"

Amber blinked and sighed with relief. She didn't want a burnt mouth! With all the worry, she'd forgotten what Chloe had told them as soon as she'd said it.

"So what do we do now?" Erin asked. It'd been bothering her all the way here. They had to stop Trudge somehow.

Kayla flapped one of her floppy brown ears. "Perhaps Trudge will stop all by himself? After all, he only started today. Maybe he'll realize he's being horrible and start behaving himself by tomorrow."

"Maybe," Chloe replied. But her wings dipped, as if she didn't seem very sure.

The raspberry bush suddenly shook, making the puppies jump. "Hello?" a voice outside boomed.

Amber leapt up from the table, shaking. "Oh, no, it's Trudge. He's come to find us!"

But Kayla frowned. "That doesn't sound like Trudge's voice. His was more . . . growly, I think."

Chloe flew upwards. "I'll go and take a look. You puppies stay right there." The butterfly fluttered towards the entrance and Erin couldn't help but follow her.

"I won't let Trudge see me," Erin told Kayla and Amber when she saw them giving her funny looks. The Labrador scampered behind the butterfly while the terrier and the cockapoo pricked up their ears so they could hear what was happening outside.

"Oh, hello, Trim," Chloe's voice fluttered. "How can I help you?"

Back inside the raspberry bush, Kayla nudged Amber. "I knew it wasn't Trudge!" she mouthed.

"I'm extremely sorry to bother you, especially in your home," came the new troll's voice. "But I wanted to apologize for my son's behaviour. I just don't know what to do about him!"

Amber and Kayla heard Erin introduce herself to Trim, Trudge's mother. "Let's go and meet her too," Kayla said, feeling strange now that they were hiding inside Chloe's home. So the two puppies scrambled out of the hedge. Outside stood a troll who looked almost exactly like Trudge, with large grey ears, green eyes and brown dungarees, except she had short hair and blue laced shoes.

Trim smiled at Amber and Kayla, and they introduced themselves.

"Do you know why Trudge is demanding something from everyone who wants to cross the bridge?" Erin asked Trim, her golden head tilted to one side.

"I'm afraid not," the troll replied. "He doesn't need any of the things that the creatures are giving him. I don't understand," she sighed. "We've spent so long changing creatures' views about what trolls are like and now Trudge is ruining our reputation. We care about others, really. Chloe will tell you – right, Chloe?"

The butterfly nodded solemnly. "The trolls of Blossom Meadow are some of the kindest I know!"

"As trolls, our job is to guard crossing points and keep them safe," Trim continued. "Not to ask for bribes from anyone who wants to use them. You mustn't think badly of us!"

"We believe you," Kayla said, giving Trim a sympathetic smile.

Trim smiled back. "Thank you. You are just as nice as the fairies told us you were!"

"You know about us?" Erin blurted out.

"Oh, yes," Trim said. "Bran told us you helped them out with a problem, although he wouldn't say exactly what. And so I was wondering, since you helped the fairies, would you be able to help us with Trudge? We don't know what else to do. Otherwise, I fear we'll have to send him away from Blossom Meadow!"

Chapter 5

The Trouble
With Trudge

Trim put her big grey head into her giant
grey palms. Amber hoped she wasn't
crying.

The three puppies looked at each
other. Helping the fairies with their
bluebell problem had seemed easy
compared to this!

"Of course we'll help you!" Erin promised.

"We'll try our best," Kayla quickly added.

"We're just not sure exactly how," Amber joined in. "Erin has already tried speaking to Trudge."

Trim nodded. "I know. I saw her. I was watching on from under the bridge. And I followed you here afterwards, as you seemed so determined to help."

Amber closed her eyes, thinking. "Has

Trudge always been like this?" she asked when she opened them again.

"Oh, no," Trim said in her deep troll voice. "He's normally just as kind as the rest of us. He only started behaving badly today!"

"Chloe told us that already," Erin said to Amber, but she couldn't be annoyed about her friend forgetting again. There was so much to take in, including the fact that they were puppies not girls!

"Hmmm," Kayla said, twitching her little brown nose. "Then something must have happened to make Trudge change like this. Any ideas?" she asked Trim.

The troll shook her head. "Nothing's happened in the last few days. It's been especially quiet in the meadow."

Chloe fluttered into mid-air. "I can't think of anything either," she tinkled.

"Trudge is usually a happy troll. I often hear him singing as I pass over Buttercup Bridge."

Trim nodded to agree. "I really must go now – I left the other trolls babysitting Tippy, my youngest son."

"Leave it with us," Erin said.

"Thank you again, dear puppies. Blossom Meadow is lucky to have you!" Trim waved and walked away, each footstep making the ground tremble a little.

"Come inside and drink your tea," Chloe said. "You'll think more clearly with some raspberry goodness inside you!"

The puppies did as Chloe suggested, and slurped down their tea. Amber wasn't sure whether it would help her think better, but the delicious tea definitely made her insides feel all warm and gooey.

Erin finished her cup first and plonked it down on the table. "We really should go now," she said. "Who knows how Trudge is behaving while we sit around. We need to stop him as soon as possible!"

Amber and Kayla tipped the rest of their drinks down their throats. Erin was right. Their friend was always impatient to get moving, but today it was especially important to hurry.

"Good luck!" Chloe called, as they said goodbye to the butterfly. "See you soon, by the sun, stars or moon!"

The puppies ducked out of the raspberry hedge and back into the bright sunshine. Kayla wondered if the weather was always this warm and sunny in Blossom Meadow. The strong sunshine made every leaf, grass and flower sparkle, and she began to get very hot as they bounded across Violet Green towards the bridge.

"Let's go and watch for Trudge again," Erin panted.

"Do we have to?" Amber replied, scrunching up her sleek black face. "It's horrible seeing him being nasty to everyone."

"It's the only way," Kayla said. "But you could stay here with Chloe if you wanted to?"

"Oh, no!" Amber cried. "I'm not leaving you and Erin!"

The puppies crept back to the patch

of violets they'd hidden behind earlier. They tried to snuggle into the shade of the flowers, but the stems were low and didn't give them much shadow.

They'd only been waiting for seconds when a squirrel dashed out from a bush towards the bridge. Erin had to bite her lip not to warn the animal, but she knew they couldn't give themselves away.

Sure enough, as the squirrel grew closer, Trudge flung himself from the river up on to the bridge.

"Payment for your crossing!" he bellowed.

The squirrel paused, then looked left and right, as if she might find another way to get across the stream. She took a couple more steps forward. "I just have this acorn," she said, lifting it up in both paws. "But surely you don't want that. Trolls don't eat acorns!"

Trudge growled and stared at it. "No, we don't, but it looks pretty. I'll take it!" He held out his hand and the squirrel reluctantly handed it over, mumbling something under her breath.

She hadn't even reached the other side of the bridge when more creatures appeared in the buttercups.

"Are they ants?" Amber whispered and Kayla nodded.

"I think so."

Erin stared at the tiny insects. "What on earth will ants have to give to Trudge?"

Amber bounced on her paws. "Oh dear, I hope Trudge doesn't stomp on them!"

But the ants were carrying a maple leaf which Trudge quickly took as payment. The ants shuffled quickly over Buttercup Bridge, looking sadly back at their precious leaf.

The puppies had to wait a while for the next creature to appear. "Perhaps word is spreading that no one should come near?" Kayla said. Eventually, a red fox with a long bushy tail approached the bridge. He was carrying a bundle of twigs, which Trudge seemed delighted with.

After the fox, no creatures appeared
for ages, and the puppies' eyes began to
droop as they grew tired in the warm
sunshine.

"We could go back to Chloe's for some
more raspberry tea?" Amber said, blinking
furiously to stay awake.

But then, Kayla's floppy brown ears
pricked up. "Wait, what was that?" she said.

Amber and Erin listened carefully. Kayla
was right. There was a mumbling noise
coming from the bridge. It was Trudge! He
hadn't jumped down off the bridge after
the fox had passed, and was sitting slumped
against the railing.

"Stupid baby brother," Trudge
grumbled. "Everything was great until
Tippy was born. Stupid, stupid Tippy."

The puppies looked at each other. "Trim
mentioned something about Trudge having

a younger brother, didn't she?" Erin asked.

"Hmmm, but she said nothing had happened recently," Kayla said. "Tippy couldn't have just been born."

"But it sounds as if that's what's upsetting Trudge," Amber added.

Erin frowned, remembering something. "When my sister Phoebe was born, I pretended to be happy, but deep down I didn't like it because no one seemed to care about me any more. One day, when she was about one year old, I started being naughty."

"Like Trudge is doing now!" Kayla clapped her fluffy brown paws together.

"Yes!" said Erin. "I used my mum's lipstick as a crayon all over our hallway walls and tipped soap all over the bathroom floor."

The puppies couldn't help laughing.

They couldn't imagine Erin being so naughty!

They'd finally worked out what was wrong! Trudge was probably feeling left out and ignored. Kayla's smile fell. "But how are we going to make Trudge feel better? How are we going to get him to stop behaving badly?"

"I think we should talk to him again," Amber said.

Her two friends turned and stared at her in surprise. Amber hated confrontation, and here she was suggesting exactly that!

"But he didn't want to speak to me last time," Erin said. "And he sounds even more upset now..."

Kayla was tapping her paws on the ground, thinking it over. "I guess there's no harm in trying. We could ask him even more nicely to stop."

Amber shook her head, making her ears flop from side to side. "No, that's not what I mean. What if we went to chat to him – get him talking about other things, rather than what he's doing on the bridge? That's what my mum does when I'm upset. She talks to me about other things, and it helps me to realize what's really wrong."

"Amber, you are so clever!" Erin said. "I'd never think of that!"

Kayla nodded and wagged her tail. "Let's go and try!"

The puppies crawled out of their hiding place and walked slowly towards the bridge. They waited for Trudge to pop up and shout at them, but he stayed slumped on the bridge.

"Hello," Erin called out when they reached the carpet of buttercups. It reminded her of the red carpets celebrities walked over at film premieres – except this one was yellow and led to an unhappy troll!

"What are you doing here again?" growled the troll. "Leave me alone!"

Chapter 6

Fairy Fun

Amber backed away. "Maybe this isn't such a good idea after all," she whispered to her friends.

"No, it's a brilliant idea!" Kayla told her. "We haven't even tried to talk to him yet."

"Let's sit down," Erin suggested quietly, and they sank gently on to the buttercups, taking care not to squish any. "We've just

come for a chat," Erin said in a louder
voice.

The troll looked over. "Why?"

"W-we're curious," Amber began.
"About living in Blossom Wood... How
long have you been here?"

"I've lived here my whole life," sniffed
Trudge. "It's the best place ever. Everyone's
happy and friendly and kind..."

Kayla shuffled a tiny bit closer to the
troll. "But you don't seem very happy right
now."

Trudge hung his head. "I *was* happy.
Then..."

"Then what?" Erin pressed, moving to
sit beside Kayla.

"Nothing. You won't understand. You're
just puppies!"

"You don't know that," Amber said,
bouncing on her paws. "We have problems

too. I don't think anyone can be happy *all* the time. And that's OK. But it's always better to talk about it."

Trudge turned so he was facing the puppies. His eyes looked big and sad. "It's my brother, Tippy," he said quietly. "Ever since he was born, no one cares about me. Not just my mum, but all the other trolls too. They say I'm old enough to look after myself – and I am. But it would be nice for them to be interested in what I'm doing sometimes."

Kayla tiptoed even closer to Trudge, and put her paw gently on his big green shoe. "I'm sure they do care really. Have you told them how you feel? Maybe that would help…"

A tear dripped off the end of Trudge's grey nose. "I can't. They'll think I'm being horrible! He's my baby brother, after all.

I pretended to be happy when he arrived,
because I knew that was what everyone
wanted. So they won't believe me now if I
tell them the truth!" The troll took a deep
breath and began to sob.

Oh no, thought Amber. *Poor Trudge!* She
walked forward and nestled her head into
Trudge's side. "They'll understand. And
they won't think you're a liar. They'll only
think that you were trying your best."

A splashing sound came from below
them. The next moment, five trolls of all
shapes and sizes flipped up on to the bridge.

"Trudge!" said Trim, rushing over to hug her son. "I heard what you said. I'm sorry. I should have paid you more attention."

"Us too," added the rest of the trolls, crowding around him.

The smallest troll, barely taller than the puppies, looked up at Trudge. "Do you hate me?" he asked, his troll voice much higher than the others.

Erin nudged Kayla and Amber. "That must be Tippy!" she whispered.

Trudge stared at Tippy for what seemed like hours, but was probably just a few seconds. Finally, he said, "No, I don't hate you. I like having a younger brother to play with. I love you! But..."

"You don't want to be forgotten," his mum, Trim, finished for him.

Trudge nodded. "I'm sorry for being

horrible to everyone who wanted to cross the bridge. I didn't really like doing it. I don't know why I did. . ."

"I think I do," Trim said. "It was the only way you could get us to notice you." She looked at her son with serious eyes. "But if we promise to pay you more attention, will you promise to let creatures pass over the bridge in peace? You're giving trolls a bad name after all we've done to ensure creatures think well of us."

Trudge gazed around at the trolls. "Yes. I

promise. I'm sorry!" He stood up and back-flipped off the bridge without another word. The next moment, he flipped up again, this time with a bundle of objects in his grey hands. "I'll go and return everything right now." With one last smile at the trolls, he ran off into Violet Green, his heavy footsteps making the ground tremble.

Trim was beaming from pointy ear to pointy ear. "Thank you, puppies! I knew you'd be able to help. Now, is there anything we can do to say thank you?"

The puppies looked at the bridge, crowded with trolls. They still couldn't cross it – there were too many towering trolls in the way!

"There is something," Kayla began. She didn't want to seem impolite by leaving the trolls already, but they had waited a long time to visit the fairies!

"Anything!" Trim said.

"We'd just like to get across!" Erin blurted.

"Oh!" the trolls cried together, looking at one another. Some stepped to the left, and some stepped to the right – which meant there was still no way across the bridge. And the puppies didn't fancy their chances amongst those big troll feet. They would easily be squished!

The trolls laughed and moved again . . . but the same thing happened. The bridge was still blocked!

"OK," said Trim. "Let's *all* move left!"

With one giant step that made the bridge shake, the trolls all moved to the left. Finally, the right side of the bridge was clear, and Erin, Amber and Kayla began to scamper across.

"Thank you!" they called back once

they'd reached the other side.

"No, thank *you!*" shouted the trolls, before leaping back down to their home under the bridge.

The puppies raced along Lupin Lane towards Bluebell Grove. With any luck, they wouldn't have missed the fairy twins' birthday party completely.

"Happy birthday!" yelled Erin when they arrived at the bluebells.

Bran and Sen, the fairy twins, were sitting cross-legged making daisy-chains. They looked at the puppies with confused frowns on their blue-tinged faces.

"Oh dear, are we too late?" Amber asked. "I'm so sorry!"

"Sort of," said Bran. "Our birthday was last week!"

"Oh!" said Kayla. *Time must pass differently here compared to back home*, she thought. "I mean, we came to wish you a *belated* happy birthday." No one in Blossom Meadow knew that the puppies came from somewhere else entirely, and Kayla had a feeling it would be best if it stayed that way.

"Did you have a good party?" Amber asked, a bit disappointed that they'd missed it. She'd been hoping for some more of their magical fairy cake!

Sen and Bran nodded. "It was perfect!"

Bran said. "We had games and cake and fairy pop and dancing."

"We missed you, of course," Sen added, smiling at the puppies. "But at least you're here now!"

Suddenly Bran leapt into the air. "I know, let's have another party, as you missed out on the last one!"

Moments later, the twins had gathered all the fairies from their home in the

bluebells. Each one seemed to have a party item ready and waiting! One fairy hung rainbow bunting all over the bluebells, and another brought out a lily leaf piled with blue cupcakes.

Then a circle of purple toadstools appeared and they played Musical Toadstools, while three fairies sang songs about sunshine and flowers and magic. The puppies had a great time – although the toadstool chairs were a *little* small for them!

Next they drank blueberry cordial, made flower garlands and danced the conga with their fairy friends. They played Pin the Chestnut on the Tree, and Fairy Says, and Pass the Poppy. Erin, Amber and Kayla had never done so much at one party!

By the time they'd finished all the games, the sun was setting, shining a pinky glow all across the meadow.

The fairies began to leave the party. Erin remembered Bran telling them before that fairies had to go to bed at dusk to recharge their magic.

"I think we should probably get going now," Kayla said to the twins, not wanting to make the tired fairies stay up too late.

Amber and Erin nodded. "It's been brilliant fun," Erin said, beaming.

Despite being tired, Amber hopped up and down with happiness. "Thank you for putting on a party just for us!"

"There's just one last thing we want to do before you go," Sen said, and the fairy twins fluttered over to tickle each puppy on the ear.

This must be how they hug! thought Erin, as Amber giggled uncontrollably. Her ears were very ticklish – both as a girl and as a dog!

Then Kayla spotted glowing blue dust in

the air around them. She followed it with
her nose. It smelt of flowers!

"That's fairy dust we've just sprinkled over
you," said Sen. "It'll give you good luck!"

Erin, Kayla and Amber waved goodbye
to the fairies as they disappeared into the
bluebells. Amber took off the collar she'd put
around her neck for safekeeping. The friends
knew that when they held it together, it
would transport them back home.

I'm not sure we can get much luckier, Amber
thought, as they clutched the collar tightly

and felt the familiar tingle of magic. *We've had another amazing adventure in Blossom Meadow, and I can't wait for the next one!*

BFF

Did You Know?

 George the badger certainly loves cake, but other badgers mainly eat earthworms and occasionally have fruits and flower bulbs.

Deer are part of the *Cervidae* family of animals. The *Cervidae* family includes moose, elk and reindeer.

You might remember the family of tawny-brown mice from the story. As a group, mice are known as a "horde" or "mischief".

 Foxes have amazing hearing — they can hear a watch ticking from around 30 metres away!

Word Search

Can you find the names of five flowers
that grow in Blossom Meadow?

B	L	U	E	B	E	L	L	S	X
J	F	B	L	U	R	J	I	T	U
V	G	H	J	T	V	K	U	P	I
I	D	O	I	T	K	O	T	O	S
O	A	D	F	E	H	L	H	P	X
L	I	A	B	R	J	Q	E	P	R
E	S	C	U	C	E	P	Y	I	C
T	I	D	F	U	J	R	F	E	L
S	E	G	H	P	E	A	E	S	O
U	S	T	B	S	E	T	S	N	Z

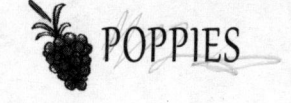 BLUEBELLS DAISIES  BUTTERCUPS

POPPIES VIOLETS

Spot the Difference

Can you spot five things that are
different in these pictures?

Amber Fact File

Want to get to know Amber better?
Here are some fun facts about her. . .

Name: Amber

Age: 9

Family: Lives with her mum (no brothers
or sisters)

Favourite dog: Dachshund

Transforms into: Terrier

Favourite hobby: Playing football

Favourite book: *Anisha, Accidental Detective*
by Serena Patel

Likes: Sports and
being outdoors

Dislikes: Being
asked for directions,
as she can never
remember them!

Party time!

Can you help Kayla, Erin and Amber get to the fairy twins' birthday party on time?

Meet

The Owls of Blossom Wood

in these magical books

Meet
The Unicorns of Blossom Wood

in these magical books

Read on for a sneak peek of
the first book in the series!

Catherine Coe

Super cute puppy games
and quizzes inside!

BLOSSOM

The
Puppies of
Blossom
Meadow

Fairy Friends

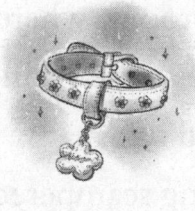

Chapter 1

Doggy Delight

"This is nothing like I thought it'd be!"
Erin said, as she, Amber and Kayla stepped
through the front door of a red-brick
Victorian house.

Kayla nodded. "It's just like a home,
right? Not like a dog kennels at all. I mean,
apart from all the dog toys, dog collars and
dog baskets!" Kayla joked. They stepped

into the main room, where dogs of all shapes and sizes were sitting in dog baskets and on covered sofas.

A sausage dog scampered up to Amber, and she knelt down to stroke its sleek, brown fur. "Hello, Matt," she said, reading the dog's name tag. "Aren't you friendly? But I've never heard of a dog called Matt before!"

Kayla's dad stepped into the room behind them. "Oh, we get all sorts of dog names here," he said. "The biggest problem is remembering them all!" Kayla's dad worked at Doggy Delight, and she'd visited before, but this was the first time Kayla had been allowed to bring along her two best friends. She'd pleaded with her dad for ages to let the three of them help out at the kennels, and at last he had decided they were old enough. They were SO excited at the thought of spending the whole day surrounded by cute dogs.

"This one's my favourite," said Kayla, stroking a German Shepherd with a very pink and waggly tongue. "Poppy comes here every day while her owners are at work. Can we take her out for a walk, Dad?"

"Not yet," Kayla's dad replied. "But the three of you can come out with me later, when it's time for the mid-morning walks."

Amber hopped from foot to foot with excitement, while Erin punched the air, shouting, "Awesome!"

The three friends lived in the same tower block, twenty minutes' walk from the kennels, and they weren't allowed any pets in their flats. But Erin had loved animals ever since she was a baby and had spent summers on her grandparents' farm in

Sweden, helping to look after the sheep and hens. She knew she wanted to work with animals one day, and now she was getting the chance to try it out!

"First," Kayla's dad said, "please could the three of you clean out the storeroom? It's been ages since it was tidied."

Amber, Erin and Kayla looked at each other. Cleaning wasn't exactly what they thought they'd be doing today!

"OK, Dad," Kayla said. "As long as you promise we can take the dogs out for walks once we're done?" She gave him a wide, pleading smile.

He laughed. "Sure thing," he said. "The storeroom's in the shed at the end of the garden. Here's the key."

The three best friends made their way through the house to the back door, stroking the dogs they passed as they went.

Outside, the narrow garden was full of dog obstacles and toys. Amber skipped over a series of agility bars laid out on the grass, while Kayla and Erin walked along the stone path.

"I didn't know dogs did the hurdles too!" Amber said, panting. The hurdles was her favourite race at sports club.

She was about to try squeezing through a training tunnel when Erin called out, "Come on, Amber! The quicker we can get the storeroom cleaned, the quicker we can get back to the dogs."

Amber skipped over to her friends as they reached the storeroom. Kayla unlocked the padlock on the door and they stepped into the room. The air inside danced with specks of dust that sparkled in the sunshine coming through the window.

"ACHOO!" Kayla sneezed.

Erin looked around at the shelves crowded with dog accessories and the piles of cardboard boxes on the floor. "Your dad wasn't joking when he said it hadn't been tidied for a while!" she said to Kayla.

"I thought it'd only take a few minutes," said Kayla, sighing. She retied the two topknots that kept her black curly hair in place and offered an extra hairband to Amber. Her friend smiled gratefully and pulled back her long, brown hair into a ponytail.

Erin tucked her bobbed blonde hair behind her ears and knelt down to start on the first shelf. She began tidying the bags of dry dog food and cleaning up the spilled pellets with a dustpan and brush.

"Ooh, look, a cuddly chicken!" Amber cried, pulling down a soft toy from the top shelf. As she grabbed it, the chicken made a giggling sound. "Is it supposed to make dogs laugh?" she wondered.

Erin shook her head as she kept on cleaning. "It's for puppies to chew on, I think. It stops them from chewing on furniture."

Kayla jumped up to reach the shelf and grabbed a chicken in each hand. She shook them like maracas and started singing, "Chick, chick, chicken! Ch-ch-ch-chick, chick, chicken!" Her friends laughed as she sprang around the storeroom.

"What's this?" Amber asked, after Kayla had stopped dancing.

Erin looked up at the short green rope in Amber's hand. "That's a tug toy. My uncle's Labrador loves playing with those."

Kayla grabbed a broom and started sweeping the floor, swishing it around as if she was dancing the waltz with it.

Erin finished sorting the dog-food shelf and moved on to the next one above it. Behind her, Amber opened a cupboard filled with dog-grooming supplies. As she moved some brushes to the top of the cupboard so she could clean the shelf, she felt something up there, and tiptoed to grab it.

"Look!" Amber said, spinning around to her friends.

"What is it now, Amber?" Erin said. "We'll never get this done if you keep stopping to look at stuff!"

Kayla swept over to Amber to take a look. "It's just an old collar."

"Maybe . . ." Amber said. "But it looks different." She blew the dust off the collar and the purple fabric sparkled.

Erin came over to see it too. "Blossom," she said, reading the name tag. "That's a

lovely name for a dog."

Kayla frowned. "Dad's never mentioned a dog named Blossom being here. And he tells me about *all* the dogs that come to stay."

The shiny silver name tag spun around on its chain, and Erin and Kayla reached out at the same time to hold it still again.

"Did you feel that?" Amber asked, looking down at their hands on the collar. It was suddenly tingling and warm, as if it were alive. The next moment, white sparkles started bouncing out from the collar and whirling around in the air, like they were surrounded by a beautiful spinning firework.

Erin let out a shriek as her feet lifted, and she saw Amber and Kayla were rising up too. The three friends stared at each other as they were whisked upwards, their eyes wide and amazed. Soon they were surrounded by so many sparkles that they couldn't see the storeroom any more!

"What's happening?" Kayla yelped as she gripped the trembling collar.

"I don't know!" Erin gasped. "But hold on tight!"

 Would you like more animal puzzles and activities?

 Want sneak peeks of other books in the series, including the Owls and Unicorns of Blossom Wood?

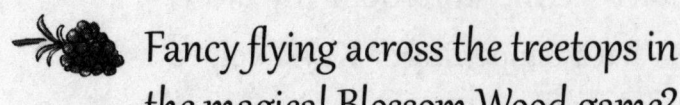 Fancy flying across the treetops in the magical Blossom Wood game?

Then check out the Blossom Wood and Blossom Meadow website at:

blossomwoodbooks.com